Nene's Balancing Notes

Ancel Mondia

Ukiyoto Publishing

All global publishing rights are held by

Ukiyoto Publishing

Published in 2023

Content Copyright © Ancel Mondia

ISBN 9789360490775

*All rights reserved.
No part of this publication may be reproduced,
transmitted, or stored in a retrieval system, in any form
by any means, electronic, mechanical, photocopying,
recording or otherwise, without the prior permission of
the publisher.*

The moral rights of the authors have been asserted.

*This is a work of fiction. Names, characters, businesses,
places, events, locales, and incidents are either the
products of the author's imagination or used in a fictitious
manner. Any resemblance to actual persons, living or
dead, or actual events is purely coincidental.*

*This book is sold subject to the condition that it shall not by
way of trade or otherwise, be lent, resold, hired out or
otherwise circulated, without the publisher's prior
consent, in any form of binding or cover other than that in
which it is published.*

www.ukiyoto.com

Contents

PEACE & CHAOS	1
YOUTH & OLDNESS	2
WEALTH & POVERTY	3
LOVE & HATE	4
PRIDE & SHAME	5
CHARITY & GREED	7
PATIENCE & WRATH	8
DILIGENCE & SLOTH	9
FREEDOM & OPPRESSION	11
CLEANLINESS & FILTHINESS	12
CONNECTION & SOLITUDE	13
PLEASURE & PAIN	14
CREATION & DESTRUCTION	15
SECURITY & DANGER	17
TRUTH & FANTASY	18
GRATITUDE & JEALOUSY	20
HEALTH & SICKNESS	22
REASON & EMOTION	23
SUCCESS & DEFEAT	25
EQUALITY & DISCRIMINATION	27

ACTIVITY & STAGNATION	29
EASINESS & DIFFICULTY	31
OBEDIENCE & REBELLION	32
PATTERN & RANDOMNESS	34
FORGIVENESS & GRUDGE	36
CLARITY & AMBIGUITY	38
SIMILARITY & DIVERSITY	40
ACCEPTANCE & REJECTION	42
HAPPINESS & SADNESS	44
BEAUTY & UGLINESS	46
ENDURANCE & SURRENDER	48
CERTAINTY & DOUBT	50
WISDOM & IGNORANCE	52

PEACE & CHAOS

We are incapable of perceiving the value of peace unless we have experienced the truth of chaos. Upon dwelling in a chaotic situation, we begin searching for a peaceful state of being. However, we ought not to instantly escape chaos because it shall only keep haunting us, as peace remains distant. We ought to learn from chaos to find the way out which ultimately leads to peace. When we attain peace, it shall still be tested by chaos every now and then. The solution is to prioritize peace over chaos. We may fall short but at the end of the day we ought to bounce back by preferring peace to chaos all over again and again regardless.

YOUTH & OLDNESS

We often think that we can only be either young or old at a human time. If we are in our youth in the physical world, we cannot think in an aged manner. And if we are in our old age, we cannot act in a childlike way. However, opposites cannot exist without the other in a broad spiritual sense. Youth ought not to be associated with beginning only and oldness with ending alone. They come in as a pair in every individual. As they both hold the tendency to surface as an extreme, it is in our capacity to balance them. We cannot be absolute young nor old as youth and oldness are a fluid duality. Youth and oldness in us exist side by side as we go on with life. And it depends on us how to turn them into a good combination of our identity.

WEALTH & POVERTY

We normally associate wealth with tangible stuff we obtain while poverty with the lack of ownership. So we typically work to accumulate material things we possess to be labeled wealthy. And we deny our state of want for we despise the notion of getting classified as poor. But wealth can come in a different form as we can be financially independent but fail to feel abundant because we turn into slaves of money. And poverty can appear as a blessing that brings us back to our dependence with the ultimate source because we are definitely incapable of having all on a physical level. We ought to be aware that material stuff are moving energies that can be destructive or sustaining, so we better moderate them rather than letting them run us, because at the top of money remains humanity.

LOVE & HATE

We have known that the source is love and the culprit is hate. We naturally hold love within but because of our human state, we normally project hate. We become estranged from love that is us, so we act in ways we term hate. However, when we assess hate at its occurrence, we learn that it is actually love in its denied form. We hate ourselves because we love us to the point that we aim for our betterment. When we finally recognize hate as love, we become understanding and accepting. We perceive ourselves through the lens of love amid hate. We understand the love behind hate, and we accept hate as the sign of love. We hate because we love.

PRIDE & SHAME

We have come to understand that nobody can be alone all the time. We need one another as our existence cannot be truly separated from the rest. We have become used to believing that we all are one to the point that our actions towards self are also our actions towards others. However, the idea of union has been exaggerated until it turns out misinterpreted. We have been hesitant to be different from others because of shame which we think of as a thing that destroys us. So we have conformed with others to be considered everybody's pride which we think of as a thing that builds us. It has become normal among us to lead a shame-based or prideful lives where we eventually lose ourselves because it has never been about us but them. We have felt empty because we have forgotten that we can never be somebody to others unless we are ourselves. When we are nobody, we can never be in a union. The concepts of pride and shame only exist when we have based our character on others as our references. However, when we define ourselves from within, both pride and shame become nonexistent because we have begun to be aware that our union means being one as the universe.

CHARITY & GREED

We have been glorified for being charitable, and condemned for being greedy. But we ought to know that charity and greed are not merely about our relationships. They primarily entail our character and motives. We ought to understand that charity is about sharing and not about wasting our resources. When we give for charity, it isn't supposed to mean that we don't expect anything in return. We expect the good to be multiplied in a larger scale where we are part of, and we experience the good together. Through charity we obtain a sense of purpose and fulfillment as a collective. On the other hand, greed isn't only about receiving all the time. We can give for greed when our motive is self-serving. When we give in order to be given back in a direct and exclusive manner, our action isn't truly for others but ourselves. When giving is done for us to take advantage of others, we are being greedy. But when giving is done for the sake of the common good including us, we are being charitable. We ought to be aware that charity and greed are states of being that extend to relationships, not how we make relationships look.

PATIENCE & WRATH

We have been advised to demonstrate patience and to avoid wrath. Because with patience, we are able to stay sane and calm. While with wrath, we can't help but get worried and exhausted. When we become wrathful, we begin to think that we can control all by our flesh. Wrath rushes us to do everything but at the end, we come to realize that we haven't really done anything. But when we become patient, we begin to surrender to divine timing or intervention. Patience comforts us that the pace and plan of the universe are always better than ours. With wrath, we are stuck in our head thinking of what's ahead so we miss the present. But with patience, we learn to live in the moment that eventually unfolds our future. Because of wrath, we see delays so we wish to take shortcuts. But because of patience, we see nows so we make the most out of life. So each instance we feel like having wrath, let's remind ourselves of patience.

DILIGENCE & SLOTH

We have been told to be diligent by working hard and tirelessly. We have been made to believe that diligence is the way to productivity and success. We have based our sense of importance on the manner we demonstrate diligence. So we condemn the concept of sloth. We have been made to think that being slothful is being overly dependent and even worthless. We have been told that we can only be a source of shame and example of failure if we become slothful. We tend to forget that diligence can't always result in productivity and success. Diligence can also lead to burnout and failure because not all things can be achieved through physical effort. We have been judged for being slothful when we opt to sit or slow down or even rest. But we can benefit from sloth as we recharge ourselves and refresh our perspectives. We can also achieve something by being slothful because we can actually think. We are able to remind ourselves that some things need mental effort. Because there are times that it's not only the heaviness and constancy of the work that matter. But also, the idea that drives and the quality that makes up the work. So, we ought to know how to have both diligence and sloth to produce results.

FREEDOM & OPPRESSION

We have been trying to make freedom real, but we have been stuck in oppression. We have thought that we are acting for freedom, but we may actually be acting for oppression. We tend to forget that we can't free others because all we can really free is ourselves. Others free themselves by themselves too. When we assume we can free others, we actually oppress them. We can never define their freedom for them. Freedom is an existence from the inside individually, and oppression is a force from the outside of self. So our act towards others that tends to control them is oppression. But when we stop intervening others, they begin to find their freedom. And by simply perceiving the realization of their freedom, we help obliterate oppression. On the other hand, when others try to oppress us, it's good for us to turn inward to live our freedom. Because freedom is an existence to be sustained, as oppression has been relentless. Freedom is individuality, so let others be themselves, as we let ourselves be us.

CLEANLINESS & FILTHINESS

We have been conditioned to condemn filthiness and to glorify cleanliness. As if being filthy is unforgivable and unchangeable. And as if being clean is righteous and permanent. We tend to forget that our physical bodies produce wastes perceived as filthiness which is naturally part of us to continue to exist. However, as we continually produce wastes, we also repeatedly clean ourselves. And the coexistence of filthiness and cleanliness reminds us that no one is fully filthy or clean. Human experiences normally include the concept of filthiness which in truth even results in cleanliness. We have made ourselves dirty as we work on our worldly lives but in the end we purify ourselves as we return to our spirituality. Filthiness and cleanliness exist together to humble us with the wisdom that we cannot judge another as filthy or clean because like them, we are also both filthy and clean. Filthiness and cleanliness are a never-ending exchange taking place in our existence.

CONNECTION & SOLITUDE

We have thought that we ought to stay connected all the time because we are social beings that are supposed to be available for one another. But we tend to forget that connection at its extreme turns into codependency. We have thought that we ought to be left alone for life because we wish to prevent everybody else from hindering us from being independent. But we tend to forget that solitude at its extreme turns into melancholy. So we ought to know when to choose connection and when to choose solitude. Too much sense of being connected makes us lose our sense of self. While too much sense of being solitary makes us lose our sense of belonging. So we better connect with individuals that are like us in terms of having lives of our own yet sharing our lives with one another. We ought to connect with individuals that are not codependent and also can be solitary without getting melancholic. And we ought to be the individuals that maintain both the connection and the solitude healthy and fair for ourselves and others.

PLEASURE & PAIN

We tend to choose pleasure over pain because in pleasure we enjoy, but in pain we suffer. We normally want only the good things in life, so we always wish for pleasure. And we typically dislike all the bad things in life, so we repeatedly avoid pain. But pleasure and pain are a duality that contributes to each other's existence. Pleasure and pain intensify each other's meaning in life. All the good things associated with pleasure have their value because of the existence of all the bad things associated with pain, and vice versa. We cannot really perceive and comprehend the value of a reality in our life when we have not undergone both pleasure and pain with, through, and for that particular existence. As pleasure and pain are an inevitable exchange in life, we learn which definitely matters as we become persistent and consistent in sustaining the meaning of a specific reality in our life. We have been tested by pleasure and pain to come out true, and to determine, value, and keep which is true.

CREATION & DESTRUCTION

We have known that it is in our nature to create and destroy. Our creation has been equated to life and beauty. And our destruction has been related to death and misery. But we often forget that both creation and destruction are necessary to the existence of each other. When we destroy others, they have the power to convert the destruction into creation. They can create themselves anew. When others destroy us, we also have the power to start anew from what has been put into end. We turn into a new creation. As creation comes from within, we can constantly give birth to ourselves, our life projects, our realities. But as destruction occurs inside also, we can take the life of our inner child, our voice, ourselves. However it depends on us to understand that we experience destruction to pave way for another creation. We have been destroyed to move on from the past, to outgrow the old. We destroy to create rooms or spaces for the real and the present. We keep undergoing destruction to sustain creation of new ways, new ideas, new lives as we all are supposed to be our own process of destruction and creation.

SECURITY & DANGER

We often think of security as a material condition. We normally say that we ought to secure a home, a car, or a bank account. And we frequently use the expression of securing a life and securing a future. We have naturally defined danger as circumstances that occur against our security. We normally associate danger with the concept of emergency. But we come to realize that there is no such thing as absolute security. We have access to security and remain vulnerable to danger. In a profound sense, security is our faith that the universe, the Supreme Being, or whatever we believe in, will provide for us. And danger is a matter of perspective, as nothing is certain and permanent. In a deep sense, danger is when we disconnect from the source by losing our faith. Danger is when we turn into strayed and lost souls. And security is when we constantly claim that we are guided and protected by the divine. As everything has been planned from above, we ought not to move on our own flesh alone, replacing the spiritual with the material. Because we are spirits just having human experiences, and that we ought not to forget.

TRUTH & FANTASY

We normally believe that we ought to stick to our truth all the time because it is rational to do so. And we usually forbid ourselves to have fantasy because we think it makes us delusional. But we neglect parts of ourselves if we discontinue to fantasize. Because both fantasy and truth are necessary for us to go through and experience life. On the other hand, despite the confusion we undergo due to lack of clear definition of what is truth and what is fantasy, we ought to respect how we ourselves and others themselves define truth and fantasy. There can be seemingly truthful fantasy and fantasy like truth, but it is in our discernment to distinguish them. But it does not mean to forsake the one and acknowledge the other. We can experience both truth and fantasy as long as we remain aware of both. Both truth and fantasy are parts of humanity that bring us life lessons and make us utilize the meaning of existence. When the truth is too difficult to bear, we can fantasize in the meantime. But when fantasy seems to detach us from reality, we can wake up back to the truth. Truth and fantasy are blessings we ought to acknowledge and experience.

GRATITUDE & JEALOUSY

We have been trained to have gratitude because it is considered a good quality to possess. And every instance we turn away from gratitude, the tendency is we turn toward jealousy. So it turns out that jealousy is not a good quality to possess. Jealousy narrows our perspectives, while gratitude broadens our comprehension. We experience jealousy because we make our fellow human beings the standard for our identities. When we focus on what others are and want to be them, we feel jealous. But when we realize that nobody is really the standard for anybody else's identity including ours, we learn to be grateful. We experience gratitude because we know that we are equally spiritual beings that come from one source. We ought to remind ourselves that what we are becoming is not for the sake of what others are but for the purpose of fulfilling the life given to us by the source. We are alive not to compete in a material sense but to relish human experiences through having a spirit. We ought not to forget that our physical lives will never replace our spiritual existence. Jealousy turns us away from the source, but gratitude brings us back and turns us one with the source.

HEALTH & SICKNESS

We often wish one another health and we normally avoid having sickness. We have been trying to remain healthy so we can't be considered sickly. Because being healthy means being in good condition. Health makes us feel free, happy, and alive. While being sickly means being in bad condition. Sickness makes us feel constrained, sad, and miserable. So when we get sick but are able to restore our health, we experience a sense of victory, freedom, and recovery. We have associated health with strength and courage as we have fought and overcome sickness. But the time will inevitably come when we ought to surrender to sickness when our life purposes have ultimately been fulfilled, as sickness leads to natural death that brings us to everlasting life. Surrendering is the more courageous thing to act on. As we have relished health, we ought to remember that our health is for us to utilize our strength and capacity to fulfill our purposes on earth so when our time is up, we can perceive sickness as a welcome back to our spiritual home, and we can go home fulfilled and with no regrets.

REASON & EMOTION

We have been told to follow our reason and to disregard our emotion because reason makes us smart and emotion makes us dull that makes us do poor decisions. But we have also been told to listen to our emotion and silence our reason because emotion makes us happy and reason makes us critical of ourselves. What we have misunderstood is that we have both reason and emotion for a purpose. Reason is not all about winning arguments nor proving our intelligence. Reason is understanding circumstances by not aggravating them, and instead alleviating them when possible. Emotion is not all about pitying others nor getting absorbed in fickleness. Emotion is experiencing happenings by avoiding what inflicts pain, and demonstrating kindness as possible. We ought to upgrade reason to wisdom, and emotion to intuition. We ought to outgrow the mediocre concept of reason and emotion that makes us stuck as low vibrational beings. We ought to consider reason as our access to divine knowledge, and emotion as our connectivity to divine bliss. We have reason and emotion not to keep us trapped in human bodies, but to allow us to relish divinity in human experiences.

SUCCESS & DEFEAT

We have normally displayed and bragged about our successes, but hidden our defeats in shame and denial. Our pretense in link with the occurrences of our successes and defeats makes an illusion that we can only succeed and never be defeated. But whether we admit or rationalize our experiences, both successes and defeats are inevitable to take place in our lives. Because neither successes nor defeats are permanent, we are vulnerable to both as they are a fluid duality. When we succeed, it is not our end. We can aim for something bigger and higher. When we are defeated, it is not our end. We can aim for something else or different. Successes and defeats are subjective, so being successful or being defeated is not about conforming to the norms nor reaching the popular standards. Successes and defeats are personal experiences, so we ought to aim and strive for what matters to us. We ought to choose our battles because it is we that can define our own successes and defeats. We can never be successful or be defeated based on the opinions of others but on our own perspectives of successes and defeats. The important thing is we accept the facticity that both successes and defeats are temporary, so we ought to live and own our lives.

EQUALITY & DISCRIMINATION

We have been programmed to prove our superiority by making others look and feel inferior. So, we have fabricated standards that seem to separate us from the rest so we can feed our ego. Our false need and wrong use of power link to the idea of discrimination. We discriminate others due to their differences from us that actually ought to complement and interconnect us. But we instead devalue and dehumanize them and make ourselves the ideals. However, humanity ought to bring us back to our senses and morals. Discriminating others due to class, gender, age, race, and ability stagnates us and eventually devolves us. So we ought to change and perceive others as our equals. No matter how they seem to differ from us, we all come from one source. We ought to promote and sustain equality because instead of competing negatively, we ought to collaborate fairly. Instead of constructing something for ourselves alone, we ought to cooperate to make something happen and last for the collective. When we choose equality over discrimination, we become in tune with the oneness of every life. When we prefer equality to discrimination, we become in sync with the meaning of every creation.

ACTIVITY & STAGNATION

We have often been pushed to act or stay in activity because it means we are doing something, progressing, working hard, and something is really going on in our lives. So, we have avoided getting stagnated or being stuck in stagnation because we think we look like procrastinating, being lazy, lacking attainment, and living miserable lives. However, we have come to realize that when we are only repeatedly in activity, we get exhausted and meaningless because we are unable to assess our steps or actions as we come to know that it is not always the movement that matters, but also the intention and the rightness of our track or path. In the end, if we only live in activity, we may conclude that we have not really done or achieved anything. On the other hand, we can perceive stagnation in a different light as when everything seems in hiatus or pause, we can utilize the period by planning our steps or actions that we ought to take next. In stagnation we have the chance to think clearly without distractions that come from being in repeated nonstop activity. So we ought to take time to experience both activity and stagnation to not lose track, to keep our pace reasonable, and to align our aims and realities.

EASINESS & DIFFICULTY

We have often tried to measure or estimate the easiness or difficulty of things. Before we can decide to undergo something, we usually have attempted to guess the answer to whether it is going to be easy or difficult to do, to pass, or to love. If it appears to be easy, some of us are going to choose to experience it because we know it is going to be smooth, beneficial, and rewarding. However, some of us also dislike easiness because we associate it with boredom, lack of growth, and fickleness. On the other hand, if it appears to be difficult, some of us are going to choose to undergo it because we know it is going to be thrilling, surprising, and eventful. However, some of us also dislike difficulty because we associate it with hardship, lack of assurance, and drain. So the easiness or difficulty of an endeavor ought not to be the primary factor to be considered when we try to decide about something. Our decision ought to be aligned to our calling, in that way, both the easiness and difficulty cannot discourage us, instead they fuel us to take part in our chosen endeavor, to come out victorious, and to sustain glory.

OBEDIENCE & REBELLION

We have been instructed to be obedient, and not to be rebellious. Because we have been made to believe that through obedience, we can never go wrong, but through rebellion we can only harm ourselves. However, we have also been persuaded to be rebellious, and not to be obedient. Because we have been made to think that through rebellion, we can find ourselves and freedom, but through obedience we can never live life to the fullest. Nevertheless, we ought to understand that we have to know what to obey and what to rebel against. We ought to determine our principles and values to align ourselves to the appropriate and relevant actions and behaviors. If we rebel, we ought to rebel against conforming to the norms that can never identify what is in our spirits. We ought to rebel against the physical and material, to remain spiritual. If we obey, we ought to obey the word of our supreme being that points to our purpose and essence. We ought to obey the calling from the source, so we cannot be misled and defeated by worldly factors. So we ought to be clear about what matters to us to know where to embody obedience and where to embody rebellion.

PATTERN & RANDOMNESS

Some of us have been programmed to follow and continue the pattern so we can have our lives planned out or secured. However, we have also been persuaded to cut or break the pattern, so we can put an end to the vicious or destructive curse being passed on constantly or being repeated as time goes by. Some of us have been conditioned to embrace and go along with randomness so we can appreciate and handle spontaneity because life has been and shall always be unpredictable. However, we have been also advised to build and make something stable amid randomness, so we can have direction in life that seems to be about survival. Nevertheless, whether we prefer pattern or randomness, we ought to put an end to the vicious or destructive pattern, but follow and continue the pattern that is good and just. On the other hand, we ought to savor randomness because it is what life is also made of, but we ought to maintain our righteous stance in everything we encounter. We ought to create a good pattern of good randomness or a good randomness of good pattern in our lives.

FORGIVENESS & GRUDGE

We have been constantly reminded to forgive so that we can move forward freely and lightly. But we still tend to hold a grudge as we keep on remembering the seemingly unfair or unjust treatment we have received. Though we have known that to forgive is the thing we ought to do, we still opt to hold a grudge because we are inclined to react in the exact way. However, we ought to understand and accept the truth that seemingly unfair or unjust things happen to us in order for us to be redirected and to put us on the right track that is ours to rightfully take. We ought to know that grudge shall only mislead us from fulfilling our own reason for being, and rob us of the life that is actually ever present in us to live and savor. So we ought to train and practice ourselves to uphold and instill forgiveness in ourselves and lives. We ought to forgive others, circumstances, and ourselves, accepting the truth that the experience is not for us to pursue or maintain. We ought to let go of a grudge so we can make space for the things that have been laid in front of us, and which are given only for us. Grudge imprisons us in the things that are never ours, but forgiveness frees us toward the things that have always been ours.

CLARITY & AMBIGUITY

We often like ambiguity because we find the mystery and the unknown attractive and exciting. We take ambiguous things in a positive way because we believe that they keep us wondering and imagining. On the other hand, we usually dislike clarity because we think that predictability and routine are monotonous and meaningless. We perceive clear things in a negative light because we feel that they keep us stuck and stagnant. However, as we grow and mature, we begin to prefer clarity to ambiguity. We have come to realize that ambiguity creates confusion and disconnection. We begin to know that ambiguity cannot always be equated to depth and wisdom. Moreover, we have come to understand that clarity yields certainty and constancy. We begin to see that clarity cannot always be linked to passivity and inaction. As we determine the spiritual things that truly matter, we begin to give less attention to things that are ambiguous, and prioritize more the things that are clear to us. We cannot avoid questioning circumstances because of random ambiguity, but we ought to be sure of ourselves with defined clarity.

SIMILARITY & DIVERSITY

Some of us have often preferred similarity to diversity because we want something to relate with and connect to. We have hated to feel uncomfortable and adjust with the facticity of diversity. On the other hand, some of us have also preferred diversity to similarity because we want something to learn from and explore with. We have hated to feel stagnant and be stuck with the facticity of similarity. However, we ought to be conscious of the truth that diversity is a natural reality. We ought to understand that we all are a piece of diversity. What we ought to do is to respect and acknowledge ourselves and others as naturally diverse. On the other hand, we also ought to be aware of the truth that similarity coexists with diversity as a natural reality. We ought to realize that we all are interconnected through our similarity. What we ought to do is to reciprocate and balance ourselves and others as naturally similar. We ought to recognize the reality that we all are pieces of diversity, and being pieces ourselves makes us similar to one another. We may have diverse realities but we learn similar lessons that we end up considering timeless and universal.

ACCEPTANCE & REJECTION

We have been working on things, proving ourselves, and maintaining situations for the idea of being accepted. We have been spending our lives trying to present ourselves as deserving of acceptance. We aim for acceptance because it is good to feel and know that we belong somewhere and we are not alone. However, as we commit to work on things, try to prove ourselves, and intend to maintain situations, we cannot avoid getting rejected. We have been fighting for our lives trying to show ourselves unworthy of all sorts of rejection. We deny rejection because it makes us feel small and less as we see ourselves as failures. Nevertheless, we ought to understand that we are not made to be accepted in everything or by everyone, because we cannot be everything nor everyone. So we ought not to be afraid of rejection because it actually directs us into becoming the persons we ought to be, into being something or someone. Through rejection, we come to know whose acceptance matters and it is not of the ones that reject us. We are being rejected because we are meant for something else, and what is for us eventually shall accept us.

HAPPINESS & SADNESS

We tend to choose happiness over sadness because happiness brings positivity while sadness brings the opposite. We pursue and do things that make us happy because we naturally enjoy good experiences, and we avoid and undo things that make us sad because we normally struggle with bad experiences. However, if we become all about happiness or we become constantly happy, happiness itself loses its meaning and significance to our existence. We gradually learn to devalue and neglect the idea of happiness because it becomes cheap as it becomes overly accessible. We begin to believe that no matter what we do, happiness shall always be within reach and available, so we turn blind from its value. Nevertheless, as opposites exist to maintain the importance of the one and another, sadness exists for a good reason, and that is to give emphasis to the significance of happiness as well as highlight the usefulness of sadness itself. Through sadness, we lose happiness, and we realize the value of being happy at being sad ourselves. We become able to determine what brings us sadness, so we naturally shift to what brings us happiness. We learn to appreciate and prioritize happiness because we come to know that it shall be replaced by sadness when we fail to maintain happiness whose opposite is sadness.

BEAUTY & UGLINESS

We have exerted effort to look and feel beautiful because we have normally believed that beauty makes us acceptable, fortunate, and advantageous. Through our maintenance of so-called beauty, we think too highly of ourselves and exaggerate our importance to the point that we only connect with others whom we consider beautiful. However, as we cannot please and convince everybody about the beauty that we have labeled ourselves, we have struggled and denied the idea of us as looking and feeling ugly. As we have thought that ugliness makes us inferior, unlucky, and unfavored, we tend to look down on ourselves and even reject the truth of our existence. As a consequence, we condemn the idea of ugliness and push away others whom we consider ugly and we end up suffering the misery of being alone. Nevertheless, if we begin to realize the truth that beauty is only a standard and ugliness is only a judgment invented by the society whose ideas are groundless and ridiculous, we shall ignore the reality whether we are labeled beautiful or ugly. What shall matter to us is the things that bring us peace in all aspects of our beings, as we help sustain harmony with everybody else.

ENDURANCE & SURRENDER

We tend to glorify the idea and act of endurance because we often associate it with the possession and demonstration of strength. When we endure conditions, we are made to believe that we are behaving in a virtuous or righteous manner. However, when we endure, we ought to know if it is really the right thing to do and if it is worth the pain, hardship, and effort because the answer or solution is not always endurance. We ought to realize when endurance has become more of suffering and misery, it is completely reasonable for us to reconsider our conditions. When we come to understand that endurance is not the best thing to do in some conditions, we ought to freely and willingly surrender. We ought not to perceive surrender as weakness or defeat because surrender, being the right action to take, becomes the sign of bravery and freedom. When we surrender, we ought to surrender to the will and plan of the supreme being. We ought to know that enduring for worldly stuff is pointless and nonsensical, so we ought to live by surrendering to the source because by doing so, we liberate ourselves from unnecessary hardship, and begin to exist with depth and bliss.

CERTAINTY & DOUBT

When we have become overly certain about things we also become overly dependent on the idea of certainty and to the point that we abuse things by mishandling them with the certainty that tells us that they cannot detach themselves from us. However, as certainty is not designed to be misused or overused, when it is being considered in unhealthy and wrong ways, certainty is being replaced by doubt. When we have become overly doubtful about things we also become overly suspicious with the idea of doubt and to the point that we manipulate things by restricting them with the doubt that tells us that they can cut us out of their existence. So we ought to know that being overly certain and overly doubtful are not good as having excess certainty or doubt loses our sense of balance in managing our lives, and in dealing with others and circumstances. We also ought to learn that if we can be certain, it ought to be on the supreme being or on our own spirituality. We also ought to be conscious of the reality that if we can be doubtful, it ought to be on everything that goes and stands against our virtues and values. So, we ought to differentiate the things where we put our certainty and our doubt in order for us to shape our character and strengthen our intuition to make good choices in life.

WISDOM & IGNORANCE

We have often preferred to be ignorant because we believe that ignorance makes us happy and peaceful. We have glorified ignorance because we feel that being ignorant frees us from having worries and concerns. We usually opine that it is better to know less or even nothing so we can lighten or even liberate our beings, particularly our minds from all sorts of weight. As a consequence, we have avoided and condemned anything that occurs like a bringer of wisdom. As we deprive ourselves of wisdom, we deny the existence of depth and truth which are also parts of our existence. When we forsake wisdom, the reality is we also reject ourselves. We run away from the possibility of getting happier and more peaceful when we refuse to become wise. We may survive by being ignorant, but we can live by being wise. We may feel fine or okay when we are ignorant, but we can feel satisfied or fulfilled when we are wise. We may choose ignorance because we fear the more meaningful things or we simply wish to sustain the things that we are being used to. However, choosing wisdom is the thing that turns us fearless as we purposefully take part in the unfolding of entirety.

www.ingramcontent.com/pod-product-compliance
Lightning Source LLC
LaVergne TN
LVHW041552070526
838199LV00046B/1914